Walt Disney's
CINDERELLA

A Golden Book • New York
Western Publishing Company, Inc., Racine, Wisconsin 53404

Once upon a time, in a faraway kingdom, there lived a widowed gentleman and his lovely daughter, Ella. Ella was a beautiful girl. She had golden hair, and her eyes were as blue as forget-me-nots.

The gentleman was a kind and devoted father, and he gave Ella everything her heart desired. But he felt she needed a mother. So he married again, choosing for his wife a woman who had two daughters. Their names were Anastasia and Drizella.

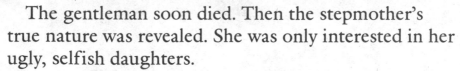

The gentleman soon died. Then the stepmother's true nature was revealed. She was only interested in her ugly, selfish daughters.

The stepmother gave Ella a little room in the attic, old rags to wear, and all the housework to do. Soon everyone called her Cinderella, because she got so covered with cinders from cleaning the fireplaces.

But Cinderella had many friends. The old horse and
Bruno the dog loved her. The mice loved her, too.
She protected them from her stepmother's nasty cat,
Lucifer. Two of her favorite mice were Gus and Jaq.
   Cinderella was kind to everyone—even to Lucifer.
But Lucifer only took advantage of her kindness.

Lucifer liked to get Cinderella in trouble. One morning, he chased Gus onto Anastasia's breakfast tray. She screamed and blamed Cinderella.

"As punishment," the stepmother said to Cinderella, "you will wash the windows, scrub the terrace, and sweep the halls. And don't forget the laundry."

In another part of the kingdom, the King was
worrying about his son. "It's time the Prince got
married!" he told the Grand Duke.

"But, sire," said the Grand Duke, "he must fall in
love first."

"No buts about it! We'll have a ball tonight. It will
be very romantic. Send out the invitations!"

When the invitation arrived, Cinderella's stepmother announced, "Every girl in the kingdom is invited to a ball in honor of the Prince."

"Why, that means I can go, too," Cinderella said.

"Well, yes," the stepmother replied with a sly smile. "But *only* if you get all your work done, and *only* if you have something suitable to wear."

Cinderella had hoped to fix her old party dress, but Anastasia and Drizella wanted her to help them, instead.

The stepmother kept her busy, too.

Cinderella worked hard all day long. When she finally came back to her little attic room, it was almost time to leave for the ball. And her dress wasn't ready!

But the loyal mice had managed to find ribbons, sashes, ruffles, and bows. The mice had sewn them to her party dress, and it looked beautiful.

The stepsisters shrieked when they saw Cinderella. "Those are my ribbons!" "That's my sash!" They tore her dress to shreds.

"Come along, now, girls," said the stepmother.

Cinderella ran into the garden. She wept and wept.

Suddenly a hush fell over the garden, and a cloud of lights began to twinkle and glow around Cinderella's head.

"Come on, dry those tears," said a gentle voice. Then a small woman appeared in the cloud. "You can't go to the ball like that. Now, where's my magic wand?"

"Magic wand?" gasped Cinderella. "Are you my..."

"Fairy godmother," the woman replied, pulling her magic wand out of thin air. "What we need is a pumpkin."

A cloud of sparkles floated across the garden. A pumpkin rose up and swelled into an elegant coach. The mice turned into horses, the old horse became a coachman, and Bruno became a footman.

"Now, off you go, dearie," said the woman.

"But my dress…" said Cinderella.

The fairy godmother looked at it. "Good heavens!" With a wave of her wand, she turned Cinderella's rags into an exquisite gown. On Cinderella's feet were tiny glass slippers.

"Now, remember," the fairy godmother said, "you must leave the ball at midnight. That's when the spell will be broken and all will be as it was before."

Cinderella promised. Then she stepped into her magical coach and was swept away to the palace.

When Cinderella arrived at the ball, the Prince was yawning with boredom. Then he caught sight of her.

Ignoring everything around him, the Prince walked over to her. He kissed Cinderella's hand and asked her to dance. They swirled off across the ballroom.

The Prince never left Cinderella's side. They danced every dance together. As everyone watched them the lights dimmed and sweet music floated out into the summer night.

And then Cinderella heard the clock begin to chime. "Oh, no!" she gasped. "It's midnight. I must go!"

"Wait! Come back!" called the Prince.

Cinderella hurried down the palace steps. In her haste, she lost one of the glass slippers, but she had no time to pick it up. She leapt into the waiting coach.

As soon as the coach went through the gates, the magic spell broke. Cinderella found herself standing by the side of the road, dressed in her old rags. On her foot, she still wore the other glass slipper.

Her coachman was an old horse again, and her footman was Bruno the dog. Her coach was an old hollow pumpkin, and her horses were four of her mouse friends. They looked sadly at Cinderella.

They all hurried home. They had to be back before the others returned from the ball.

The next day, the stepmother told the girls that the Grand Duke was coming to see them. "He's searching the kingdom for the young lady whose foot fits the slipper. Whoever she is, she will marry the Prince."

Cinderella smiled and hummed the very waltz that had been played at the ball. The stepmother became suspicious. She locked Cinderella in her room.

Gus and Jaq had a plan to help Cinderella. While
Anastasia and Drizella tried to squeeze their big feet
into the little glass slipper, the two mice sneaked into
the stepmother's pocket. They got hold of the key,
tugged it up the stairs, and unlocked the door.
Cinderella rushed downstairs to try on the glass
slipper.

"Your Grace," she said, "may I try on the slipper?"

The wicked stepmother fumed with anger. She tripped the page who was holding the glass slipper. It fell to the floor and broke into a thousand pieces.

"Don't worry," Cinderella said, reaching into her pocket. "I have the other one right here."

She put on the slipper, and it fitted perfectly.

From that moment on, everything was a dream come true. Cinderella went off to the palace with the happy Grand Duke. The Prince was overjoyed to see her, and so was the King. Cinderella and the Prince were soon married.

In her happiness, Cinderella didn't forget about her animal friends. They all moved into the castle.

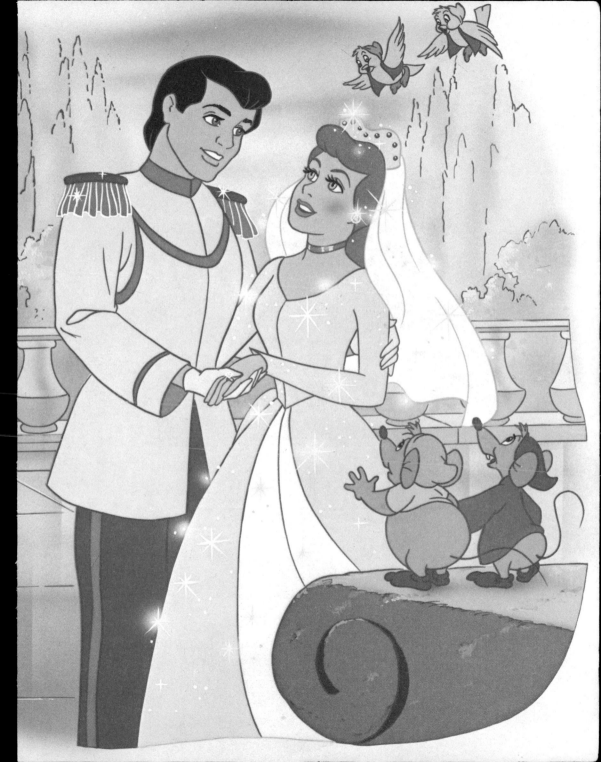

Everyone in the kingdom was delighted with the
Prince's new bride. And Cinderella and the Prince lived
happily ever after!